THE IDENTITY

JATIN ZADOO

Made with ♥ on the Notion Press Platform
www.notionpress.com

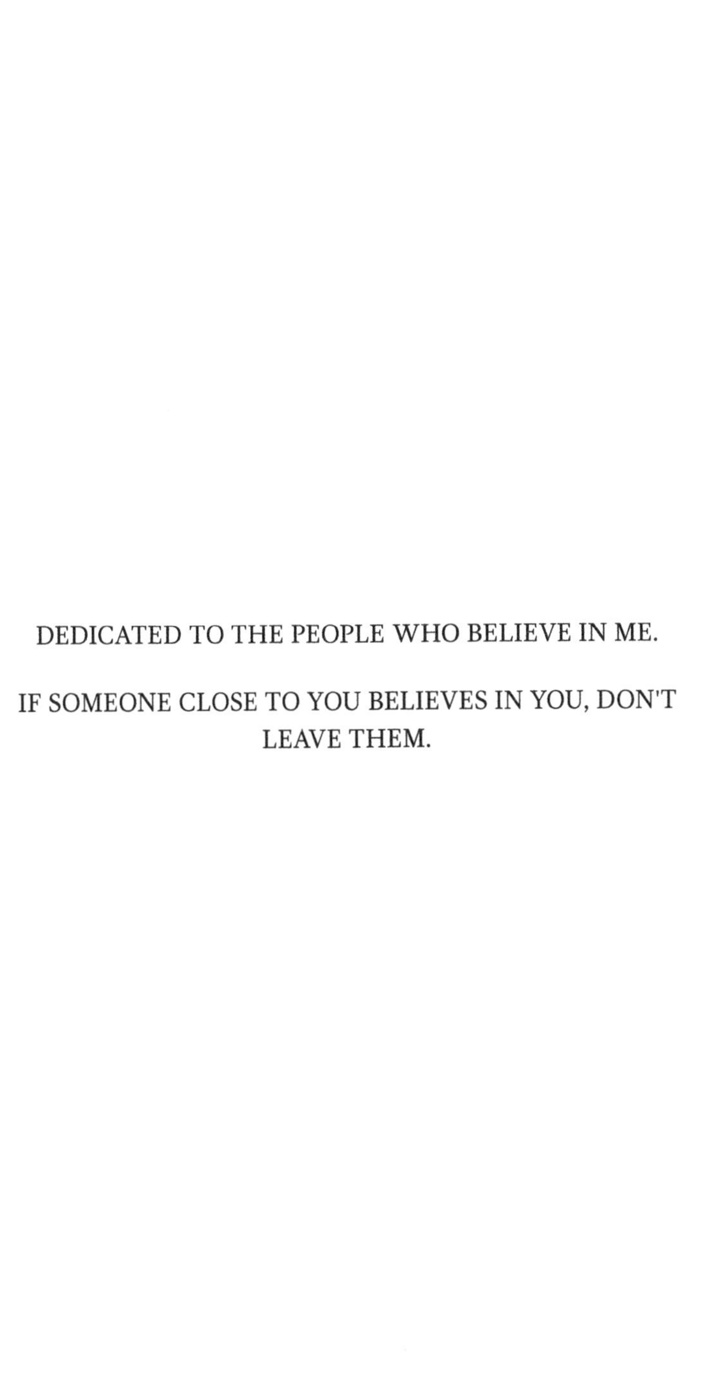

DEDICATED TO THE PEOPLE WHO BELIEVE IN ME.

IF SOMEONE CLOSE TO YOU BELIEVES IN YOU, DON'T LEAVE THEM.

Contents

Preface

" A story of a Family "

Lucy, Leo, and Ian find out that their parents are hiding something from them.

When the children find out what their parents were hiding and try to ask them, the parents disappear and they leave a message, "WE WILL COME BACK SOON."

What are Lucy, Leo, and Ian's Parents hiding?

What is the real truth?

CHAPTER ONE

KNOCK KNOCK

13th August, 8:30 a.m.

Lucy, Leo, and Ian are college students.

LUCY, LEO, AND IAN'S HOUSE

I and 'Leo' are in the second year of our college and 'Lucy' is in the final year of college.

I and Leo are in the same college, and Lucy is in a different college as she passed with the highest percentage of marks in high school.

A VOICE

Wake Up, You three, it's time for college.

This was the voice of the woman who had spent the last twenty years of her life teaching us what's good and what's bad, helping us, and worrying with and for us. But here is what she needs to understand, "No matter how early someone sleeps, waking up early is the most difficult part."

Leo: Mom, Just five more minutes.

After 15 minutes, again a voice - This time it was our father.

"Get up, Leo and Ian, and get ready for college."

We woke up.

"Only 15 minutes left before the clock strikes 9."

We finished breakfast and were waiting for Lucy.

Leo yelled, "Wake up and get ready, Lucy, you will be late for college."

Mom: Hey, stop shouting, go and sit in the car.

When we reached there, Lucy was already in the car, waiting for me and Leo.

Dad: Get in the car quickly, it's 8:55 a.m."

We sat in the car and waited for our dad to drop us at our college.

College

Not much happened during the first three lectures but when the fourth lecture started, it came with a shock, the announcement - YOUR EXAMS WILL START FROM 19th of AUGUST."

Everyone started shouting. Someone said, " We just gave..."

The teacher replied, " Be quiet, everyone. I have pinned the exam date sheet on the board outside the classroom. "

End of the Fourth Lecture

I and Leo went outside the classroom to see the date sheet.

I was checking the dates when a message popped up on my phone, "I have exams from the 17th of August." This was from Lucy.

I replied, " We also have exams but they will start on the 19th of August and will end on the 23rd of August."

FOUR EXAMS, SEVEN DAYS.

9:00 p.m.

All of us were having dinner and told our parents about the exams. They said, "Focus and try to do your best in these exams."

After finishing dinner, my father received a phone call. After the phone call, he said that they will be out for a week as one of their friends has broken his leg and so they need to visit him.

I, Lucy, and Leo said, " Okay, stay safe and try to come back as early as possible.

Our Parents replied, " We will try to."

14th August, 6:00 a.m.

Our parents left to visit their friend, and we went to sleep again.

We woke up at 10'o clock.

Lucy had already prepared the breakfast by then and we finished eating it, and then went to our rooms and started studying for the exams.

Time passed, it was now 12:30 p.m. and the doorbell rang.

DING...DONG...

Lucy: Go and see who's on the door, Ian.

I looked out from the window and said, "It's some guy in a black coat and a colorful hat."

The doorbell rang again.

Without opening the door, I said, "Who are you, mister?"

The mister replied, "I am here to give your parents a gift."

I said, " A gift, why?"

The mister replied, "Your parents are a valuable asset to our group, they are amazing."

I said, "Our parents work for a company called CP Technologies, why are you talking about a group?"

" Oh, CP Technologies, Right, Yeah, that's the name of our group. I will leave the present here near the door, tell your parents that it's from the group, oh, I mean Company." the mister replied and left.

We opened the door. There was a box.

7 Days passed

Our parents returned from their visit but like every other time, they were injured a little. When we asked about what happened, they replied, " oh, these are just scratches, don't worry about us."

Mom: So, how is the preparation going on for the last exam?"

We replied, "Still preparing."

I said, "Also, Mom, and Dad, someone came on the day you left and left a present for you and also said that you both are a valuable asset to their group/company. It's a box and it's in Lucy's possession.

Lucy: Here is the box.

Mom and Dad replied, " Oh, thanks, you three. Go and prepare for the final exam."

23rd August, 8:50 a.m.

Dad: Last paper starts in 10 minutes, get in the car, now.

Okay, Mom, we are leaving.

9:00 a.m.

Reach the college.

Dad: Do your best.

1:00 p.m.

When we reached home, there was a letter on the refrigerator, it was from Mom and Dad, we opened the letter, on it was written,

" IF YOU ARE READING THIS THEN THAT MEANS WE ARE NOT WITH YOU GUYS, DON'T TRY TO FIND US, WORK HARD AND ACHIEVE EVERYTHING THAT YOU WANT IN LIFE.

TO ALL THREE OF YOU, TRY TO BECOME THE BEST VERSION OF YOURSELVES."

Being grown-ups, we thought we will not cry but the tears were real, we were crying and yelled, " Mom, Dad,

Why, where are you" and why will you write something like this, and...?"

.

.

UNKNOWN CITY, UNDERGROUND LOCATION

"The face of the one who is talking is not visible."

He is saying, " WELCOME BACK TO THE GROUP."

Sorry but this will be a long mission for both of you. This is your 117th mission together, you two always succeed no matter how hard the mission gets but this is harder than any of the previous missions you have done, best of luck to both of you."

Let's end this with a greeting and everyone yelled,

" WELCOME BACK TO THE KILLERS, MR. AND MRS. DELLOME."

.

.

MR. AND MRS. DELLOME'S HOUSE

Lucy, Leo, and Ian are Crying.

Ian's phone rings.

RING...

RING...

The call is from an unknown number.

.

.

CHAPTER TWO

THE UNKNOWN NUMBER

RING...

RING...

Ian picks up the phone and the voice from the other side says, " Hello Ian, how are you guys, I hope you guys are okay, just don't worry about us, we will meet you again in 30 days. I don't have the time to explain everything right now."

Ian's father was the one who was calling.

Ian replies, "Huh...What're you saying, Dad? Where is Mom? Is she with you? Where are you both going,? you left a note on the refrigerator saying, "Don't try to find us, and now this, you don't have the time to explain the things that are happening, where are you?"

Ian's father replies: Your mother and I are going somewhere, we will come back, don't worry about us.

Ian was about to say something but before he could say it, Lucy yelled, " Mom, Dad, Please tell me what are you both up to this time?"

Ian and Leo: Hey Lucy, What are you saying?"

"You two don't know anything, you know when you both were young..., before she could complete the sentence, Mom yelled, "Don't say anything, Lucy."

I thought to myself, "Huh, something is wrong, Mom never calls Lucy by her name."

Lucy suddenly became calm.

The parents said, " Just focus on your college right now, and don't worry about us."

Ian replied, " Mom, Dad, but...but...Why would you write something like that (referring to the letter they found on the refrigerator), what was the meaning of that letter?"

Ian's father replied, "Don't worry about the letter, it was just a precautionary measure."

Leo: Really Dad, a precautionary measure. Tell us seriously, Dad, what's going on?

Beep...

Beep...

Beep...

The phone call ended.

UNKNOWN CITY, UNDERGROUND LOCATION

The leader of the group, the face is still hidden, " Mr. and Mrs. Dellome - Your mission will start now, your last wish was fulfilled, but I don't think this will be your last mission."

Mr. Dellome: You have promised us that this will be our last mission."

The Leader: Yeah, we will see. Let's talk about the mission first. This is just a mission in which you have to guarantee the safety of the individual no matter what happens in between."

Mr. Dellome: Yeah, we will protect the individual at all costs.

Mrs. Dellome: Yes, Don't worry about that, just keep your promise.

MR. AND MRS. DELLOME'S HOUSE

Ian: Do you know anything about Mom and Dad that we don't know?

Lucy: No, it was just...

Ian: Then what did you mean when you questioned our parents and yelled, "What are you guys up to this time." Tell us the truth, Lucy.

Lucy was about to say something but Leo's phone started ringing.

RING...

RING...

It was also an unknown number.

Ian told Leo to put the call on speaker. Leo picked up the call and responded with "Hello, Mom, Hello Dad."

But they were surprised when the voice from the other side said, " Hey kids, remember me, we met a week ago."

Leo: Oh, you are the mister from our parent's company.

The Mister: Oh, so you still remember me, so here is the message that I wanted to give - In about twenty minutes, some individuals from the police headquarters will reach your place, I guess three, maybe more"

Leo: Huh, guys from police headquarters, why?

The Mister: They will check inside and outside the house but they will find nothing.

Leo: Of course, they will find nothing. We have nothing to hide.

The Mister: Yes, they will find nothing but if I tell them where to find something, they will definitely find many interesting things, and if you want to protect your mom and dad, you should act like you normally do.

The phone call ended.

Beep...

Beep...

Leo: What's that?

Ian: Act like we normally do?

After some time, a knock on the door.

OPEN THE DOOR.

We opened the door and the individuals from the police headquarters were really outside our home, they entered our house, they searched every place (inside and outside) the house but when they failed to find anything, they asked a question, " Where are your Mom and Dad?"

We replied, "They will return in 30 days."

The individuals from the police headquarters left.

Now there were three of us with three things on our minds.

" WHO OUR PARENTS REALLY ARE?"

"WHO IS THE MISTER THAT'S CALLING US?"

"WHAT DOES THE MISTER KNOW ABOUT OUR HOUSE?"

Leo's phone rings again.

This time, he recognized the number, the Mister from the company was calling again.

Ian and Lucy: Put the phone on speaker.

Leo picked up the phone and said, "Who are you really and what do you want?"

The Mister: " Don't worry, I'm your well-wisher."

Leo: Well-Wisher, Huh... What do you mean by that?"

The Mister: If you promise me that you will protect me from your mom and dad, I will tell you everything.

Leo, Ian, and Lucy started laughing.

Leo: Mister, do you really know what you are saying, protect 'you' from our mom and dad. Don't worry, they will not kill you, they are the sweetest.

The Mister: You don't know them.

FLASHBACK OF 'THE MISTER'

The Mister is hiding near a building with dead bodies lying here and there, only two individuals are standing and one of them yells,

" WE ARE THE DELLOME'S, DON'T MESS WITH US."

THE FLASHBACK ENDS

Leo: What do you mean by 'You don't know them.'

There is a hidden basement somewhere in your house, just go to that basement and you will find a key. That key will unlock a door that will reveal everything about your parents and your family.

UNKNOWN CITY, UNDERGROUND LOCATION

"Leader, do you really want to kill them this time? Sending them on a mission like this."

The Leader decides not to speak.

Someone: This is a suicide mission.

The Leader: You are a newcomer so you don't know who they really are, they are the real founders, the real leaders of this group 'THE KILLERS,' there was a time when this whole city was filled with individuals who killed for fun, Adults with guns and ammunition. They are the reason this city is this peaceful in these present times.

Someone: But this mission is dangerous, Leader.

The Leader: Yes, for you, it is dangerous. But for them, it's a piece of cake. Don't worry about them. Focus on yourself. Maybe they will need a person like you in the later part of this mission.

MR. AND MRS. DELLOME'S HOUSE

Leo: So, where do you think our basement is?

Ian and Lucy: Shake their head.

Leo: Don't you wanna know about our family?

Ian and Lucy: No

Leo: What do you mean, No?

Lucy: I don't wanna know.

Leo: But we have to, you know, the way in which the mister was saying, I really want to know who our parents really are.

Ian: But don't you think it will be best for us not to believe the mister?

Leo: I don't want to believe the mister either but if we find a hidden basement, it will be cool, right?

Ian: What do you mean cool, how?

Lucy thinks for a second and then says, "Okay, let's find the basement."

CHAPTER THREE

WHO ARE THEY REALLY

Ian, Leo, and Lucy are thinking about where and how they can find the basement.

After a small discussion, they decide to search the whole house, they search everywhere (inside and outside the house) but find nothing.

The Phone rings again.

RING...

RING...

The call is from the mister.

This time, Ian picks up the phone call and says, "Hey Mister, were you joking when you said what you said? We searched the whole house but couldn't find anything."

The Mister: No, I was not joking. If finding it was this easy, don't you think the individuals from the police headquarters...

Ian: Yeah, we know.

The Mister: Also, you are just kids. Do you really think you will find the basement without help from someone who knows where to find it?

Ian: Yes, we are just kids, so give us a clue.

The Mister: It can wait. There is a stranger walking outside your house, deal with him, I will tell you something after that.

BEEP...

BEEP...

The Phone call ends.

Ian, Lucy, and Leo look out through the window, there was a man in a black coat with a gun in his hand.

The man in the black coat rang the doorbell.

Without opening the door, Leo said, "Who are you and why do you have a gun in your hand?"

The Man: I am a detective and I am here to meet Mr. and Mrs. Dellome. I need help from them, I have proof that there are three individuals living in this house who are working for or with 'THE KILLERS'

Ian: THE KILLERS, I have heard this name but no one here is working for or with them.

The Man: Can you call your parents, I want to have a conversation with them.

Ian: Our parents are not here right now, they said they will return in thirty days.

The man: I will leave my card here on the doormat, call me when your parents return.

The man leaves and Ian picks up the card. The card is from a detective agency titled, "LR Agency."

Leo: First the police, then the mister, and now this man. Something is wrong. Leave the card on the table, and let's search for the hidden basement again, this time let's look for things that can work as a secret mechanism. I have seen in movies that the hidden basement can be found after something attached to it is moved and after that thing is moved, a secret door opens.

The expression on Lucy's face changes !!

Lucy: I will check again inside the house, you two look for something outside the house.

After some time, Lucy calls both Ian and Leo and says, here look what I found - A key.

Leo: You found a key, Where?"

It was in the top drawer, in the kitchen.

"Now we need to find the door or a lock that gets unlocked with the help of this key."

TRAIN COACH

Mr. Dellome, Mrs. Dellome, and a stranger are in a coach, the whole coach is empty.

The Stranger: Do you know how risky this mission is?

Mr. and Mrs. Dellome: Yes, we do, but don't worry, that's the main reason we were assigned this mission - The mission of protecting you.

The Stranger: Of course, Of course, I know who you two are but returning from this mission is impossible. You know, this train is heading to a city where...

Mr. Dellome: We need to see the faces of our children again so yes we know where this train is heading to. Do you know what our city was like before the group "THE KILLERS" was founded?

The Strangers: But it's not just that.

Mr. Dellome: It was the same. Individuals who killed for fun. You could find guns and ammunition in every house but everything changed on that day. So don't worry, you are in safe hands.

Mrs. Dellome: In 13 hours, we will reach the place where this train is heading and the mission will start.

MR. AND MRS. DELLOME'S HOUSE

Lucy, Leo, and Ian are discussing where to find the lock of the key they just found.

THE MISTER CALLS AGAIN.

The Mister: Found the Hidden Basement yet?

Leo and Ian: No, but we found a key and we don't know where to find the lock.

The Mister: Oh, you found a key, and so, is the key real? Don't you think you are underestimating your parents?

Ian: What do you mean by "Is the key real" and "Underestimating your parents?"

The Mister: Do you really think that they will keep something so important in front of your eyes?

Ian: It was Lucy who found the key. Give us a clue at least.

The Mister: Oh, so Lucy found the key. I think it's the perfect time to give you a clue as this will be the last time we will talk if..."

Leo and Ian: Last time, What do you mean by that?

You will know, here's the clue;

ASK LUCY, SHE KNOWS WHERE THE BASEMENT IS.

AND ALSO ABOUT WHERE THE LOCK TO THE KEY THAT YOU WILL FIND SOON IS.

Ian and Leo (shocked): Hey Mister, are you out of your mind, First, you say that our parents are hiding something from us, now you're saying that our sister knows where the basement is? Who are you, Mister and How do you know so much about our house and family?

The Mister: It's not just the basement, your sister knows about your parents too.

Ian and Leo (another shock): What do you mean by she knows about our parents? They're her parents too.

The Mister: Ask her yourself. We will meet soon.

Ian and Leo were about to say something, but...

THE PHONE CALL ENDS.

Leo and Ian turn to Lucy and

WHAT IS THE MISTER SAYING, LUCY?

WHAT IS THE MEANING OF THIS?

BEFORE THEY COULD COMPLETE THEIR QUESTION, LUCY...

CHAPTER FOUR

WHO ARE YOU

"LUCY HITS THEM WITH A WOODEN BAT,
THEN RUNS TO HER ROOM AND TRIES TO
CALL THE NUMBER FROM WHICH THE
PHONE CALL CAME.
SOMEONE PICKS UP THE PHONE CALL,
BUT
IT'S JUST A SOUND -
BZZZZZZZZZBZZZZZZZZZZZZZZZZ
BZZZZZBZZZZZZZBZZZZZZZZZZZZZZZZ
BZZZZZZZBZZZZZBZZZZZZZZZZZZZZZZ
BZZZZZBZZZZZZZBZZZZZZZZZZZZZZZZ
BUT ..."

Leo and Ian turn to Lucy and ask her, "What is the Mister trying to say? What are you hiding from us? What do you know about our parents that we don't know? Do you know where the basement is and who our parents...?

Before they could complete the question, Lucy says, "No, No, I don't know anything, the Mister is lying, I don't know anything, I don't know where the basement is."

Leo asks Lucy: Are you lying, I don't know why but I can feel that you are lying this time. You know something, right, don't you, Lucy?

Ian: Yes, Leo, I also feel the same.

Lucy: I am telling the truth, I'm not lying, I really don't know who our parents really are. I also don't know where the basement is.

Leo and Ian: We believe you.

Leo: But then why is the Mister lying?

Lucy: Maybe he is the reason why our parents lied to us in the first place.

Leo: I don't think our parents will lie to us, but if they are lying, we need to find the answer to that question ourselves.

Ian: I will call the mister again.

Leo: Don't you think it's strange that "The Mister" knows everything about our parents and also about what's happening outside the house?

Ian: Yes, I think it's strange that the mister knows everything. I think he is nearby. What do you think, Lucy?

Lucy: Yes, I also think that he is nearby.

Ian calls the Mister, but the Mister is not picking up the phone.

A message pops up on Ian's mobile phone, Lucy is lying to you, go to her room and find the hidden door myself, and then call me.

Ian: Now the mister is telling me to go to Lucy's room and find the hidden door myself.

Lucy: There is no hidden door in my room. You will find nothing.

Leo: Let's go to your room, Lucy.

After reaching Lucy's room, Lucy says, "Go and search the room, I will wait here."

Ian and Leo enter Lucy's room and are searching for the hidden door.

TRAIN COACH

Mr. Dellome, Mrs. Dellome, and The Stranger are talking. They are now just 1 hour away from the destination.

The Stranger asks them: How are you both able to kill those monsters, don't you feel sympathy?

Mr. Dellome: You answered your question yourself. How can we sympathize with the monsters?

Mrs. Dellome: There was a time when he tried to sympathize with those monsters and lost too many people close to him or I should say someone close to him.

The Stranger: There will be approximately 100 individuals with guns and ammunition. They will start firing as soon as we reach. Do you have a plan?

Mr. Dellome: You just have to wait in this coach for approximately three hours.

The Stranger: Why?

Mr. Dellome: Part of the plan.

Mrs. Dellome: Your safety is in our hands, don't worry, we will protect you.

MR. AND MRS. DELLOME'S HOUSE

Leo and Ian come out of Lucy's room and say "We found nothing."

Lucy (yells): See, I told you, you will not find anything in my room.

Ian then replies, "Sorry for not trusting you, Lucy. I guess the mister is lying then, if yes, then why is he lying?"

A MESSAGE POPS UP ON LUCY'S PHONE.

Lucy enters her room and says " YOUR MOM AND DAD ARE NOT WHO YOU THINK THEY ARE. THEY ARE THE REASON WHY I AM HERE. I AM TRYING TO

PROTECT YOU, DON'T TRY TO FIND THE ANSWER TO THE QUESTIONS ABOUT YOUR MOM AND DAD?"

Ian (yells): Open the door, Lucy. What do you mean by "Protect you" and "Your Mom and Dad? Aren't they your mom and dad, too?

Lucy: No, they're not. The reason I am here is that when I was a kid your parents killed my parents. I never felt any anger towards them because they're the reason I became who I am today. I was about to kill myself on that day but something happened.

My parents were powerful individuals. They and their organization were the reason this city was like hell in the past. Your parents and the individuals involved with them are the reason why this city feels like home. I will tell you everything about you and your parents.

Lucy unlocks the door and looks at Ian and Leo, the truth was too much for them, the look on their faces...They were shocked after hearing the truth about their sister and also finding out that their parents are the reason, she is alive to this day. They were grateful for the life they were living right now, there were tears in their eyes.

They looked up and yelled

Thank you Mom and Dad for everything.

Leo was about to say something, but suddenly the doorbell of the house rang.

DING...

DONG...

They rushed to the door, but there was no one, only a letter,

"*MISSION 1*

DESTROY THE WEAPONS IN THE BASEMENT. LUCY WILL HELP YOU IN

REACHING THE BASEMENT. ALSO, DON'T WORRY ABOUT US, WE WILL RETURN ONCE OUR MISSION IS OVER.

FROM MOM AND DAD."

After reading the letter, Lucy says, "So, this is your first mission, but why so early, this mission is easy, you just have to destroy the weapons stored in the basement."

Leo: Are we part of the same group that our parents are part of?

Lucy: "No, not right now, but if you succeed in your fifth mission, you will become part of the group. Let's go to the basement."

Ian: I don't want to do this mission thing. Lucy, Do you know where our parents are?

Lucy: Yes, I know where they are going, they are currently on their 117th mission and as they mentioned not to worry about them, they will come back as soon as they finish their current mission and you have to do this mission. You are just destroying the weapons.

Ian: But...I don't want to.

Leo: Listen to me, Ian. Weapons are used to kill people. Sometimes innocent people. You are just destroying 0.01% or less than that of weapons.

Lucy: This is what our parents fight for. They want to see a future where no one is using weapons.

Ian: Okay, Let's go to the basement and finish the mission of destroying the weapons.

Lucy: Let's go to the kitchen and then my room. Removes the square piece from an artwork in the kitchen. (A Loud Noise) Let's go to my room now. Lucy moves the cupboard. A hidden door appears in front of them.

Leo and Ian: It was not here before when we checked.

Lucy: The magic of taking out the square piece in the artwork.

Ian gives the key to Lucy and Lucy unlocks the door. They enter the secret room.

Lucy: Find a box with a dragon on it.

Ian and Leo: Okay, there are so many things I have seen for the first time.

After searching for a while, Lucy finds the box they were looking for.

In the box, there was the key to the hidden basement.

Lucy: Let's go to the kitchen now. The door of the hidden basement is in the kitchen. It's behind the refrigerator. Lucy, Leo, and Ian move the refrigerator and unlock the door of the hidden basement and then enter the basement.

Ian and Leo couldn't believe what they were seeing, there were all kinds of weapons in the basement of their house.

Lucy: Here is the manual on how to destroy the weapons, but I know how to destroy them, so just follow me.

1...2...3...4...5...6...7....140...143...147 guns (different types)

See, this is a machine, you just have to make bends in the barrel and crush the working parts like this, now this gun is of no use.

After four to five hours of hard work, they were able to destroy all the weapons in the basement.

NEAR A BUILDING

Mr. and Mrs. Dellome are in an abandoned building surrounded by individuals with guns in their hands.

The bird-eye view of the city shows dead bodies lying in different positions with guns in their hands and the station is also filled with dead bodies.

Mrs. Dellome: 30 More to go.

Mr. Dellome: Let's finish this.

MR. AND MRS. DELLOME'S HOUSE

Lucy, Leo, and Ian are exhausted after destroying the weapons in the basement.

Leo and Ian: We are hungry.

Lucy: I will make something.

A PHONE CALL.

THEIR FIRST MISSION WAS COMPLETE BUT...

WHO LEFT THE LETTER?

WHO IS THE MISTER?

CHAPTER FIVE

MISSION 117TH ENDS WITH

"Mr. and Mrs. Dellome are currently on their 117th mission together. They reached their destination and it took them more than 3 hours to kill more than 100 monsters (in the shape of a human).

But now after killing them, they have reached a building where they are surrounded by more monsters (the ones who were left). All of them have weapons in their hands."

Mrs. Dellome: It's just like our 10th mission.

Mr. Dellome: Yeah, I remember that, let's finish this mission quickly so that we can spend our remaining time with our children. Don't you think it's too easy for us considering the fact that we were part of this situation in the past too?

Mrs. Dellome: Now, Now, don't get too over-confident, let's focus on the mission in front of us first.

GUNSHOTS

There are 30 individuals outside the building and one of them says, "They were just two and we lost more than..."

Mr. Dellome stops him and says, "Don't worry, it happens every time when we're together. (Looks at Mrs. Dellome and smiles)."

Another Individual says, "Let's go back to the leader and tell him what happened here."

Everyone yells, "Yes, yeah, let's go back."

Someone from the thirty individuals: Going back to the leader, are you out of your mind? What do you think the leader will do when we tell him that we failed to kill just two individuals and that we are the only people left? Instead of doing that, don't you think guys, they too will be feeling tired after what they have done here? Don't you think it's our chance to strike? It has been 15 minutes since they went into that build...

He was about to finish this sentence but suddenly the sound of a bullet,...

Three more...

Five more...

Seven more...

The firing stopped.

Mr. Dellome: Nice Job, Mrs. Dellome, 16 Gone, 14 Left..."

Mrs. Dellome: You too, Mr. Dellome.

Since there are only 14 left now, let's give a call to the person whose protection is in our hands and finish this mission.

OUTSIDE THE BUILDING

The remaining individuals start running. Some are trying to hide, some are just running back to the leader.

Mr. and Mrs. Dellome try to peek through the window again but there is no one outside.

They call the stranger.

RING...

RING...

He picks up the phone and his face is hidden, he says, "Were...were you able to... to kill...kill all of them?"

Mr. Dellome: No, there are still 14 left.

The Stranger: 14, you left 14 alive, are they still there, kill them.

Mr. Dellome: No, they all left, there is no one near the building, you told us to take over the building. We did that.

The Stranger: That's Good, come back to the discussed place after killing the remaining fourteen individuals and also the leader, and your mission will be over.

BEEP...

BEEP...

THE PHONE CALL ENDS

MR. AND MRS. DELLOME'S HOUSE

> "*They have finished their first mission. They are exhausted after destroying all the weapons in the basement.*"

Leo and Ian: We are hungry.

Lucy: I will make something.

Leo: Lucy, you were great. Have you fone this before?

Lucy: Yes, of course, when I was 18, this was my first mission too. Now, let's go to the kitchen and I will try to make something and then we can eat together.

Ian: But Lucy, I have a question, who is 'The Mister' and who left the letter on our doorstep?

Lucy: Maybe someone from the group left the letter and I don't know about 'The Mister' He always uses this name. Maybe he is someone from the group.

Leo: Let's talk about this when we eat, I will take a bath.

Lucy: I will make something.

Ian was about to say something but his phone rang.

RING...

RING...

Ian picks up the call

Ian: Hello, Who's this?

The person on the other side replies, " I am the leader of the group ' THE KILLERS' and I am about to tell you something strange.

YOUR PARENTS ARE DEAD.

Before Ian or Leo or Lucy could react, the phone call ended...

BEEP...

BEEP...

DISCUSSED PLACE

Mr. and Mrs. Dellome are walking towards the discussed place, holding hands, talking to each other.

Mr. Dellome: Do you really think that we should make this our last mission, you know, we were pretty cool back there.

Mrs. Dellome: Yes, for us and for our children;s sake. Let's start our life with a new start. You know, after destroying all the weapons here and then live our life comfortably - A life without fighting.

Mr. Dellome: Let's call the stra...

BEFORE HE COULD COMPLETE HIS STATEMENT, SOMETHING HAPPENED.

UNKNOWN CITY, UNDERGROUND LOCATION

The Leader of the group "THE KILLERS" is laughing.

Someone from the group: What was that, Leader? Telling the children of Mr. and Mrs. Dellome that their parents are dead, what were you thinking, leader?

The Leader (still laughing): They...Laughs...They will die...soon.

Someone from the group: What is the meaning of this?

The Leader stops laughing and says: JUST WAIT AND SEE.

CHAPTER SIX

THE THOUGHT OF LOSING A LOVED ONE

MR. AND MRS. DELLOME'S HOUSE

After the phone call between Ian and the leader of 'THE KILLERS' ended.

Lucy, Leo, and Ian start crying.

Ian: What...What is he saying? How is this possible?

Leo: No...No...It's not possible...Our Parents are dead.

Lucy: It's...It's not...possible. Dial the number again.

> "*The letter from their parents before had made them so depressed, now this phone call with the person who calls himself 'THE LEADER' saying "YOUR PARENTS ARE DEAD."*"

Ian (Tears are falling on the ground): Calls the number again. The number is not valid. How is this possible? What's the meaning of this?

Lucy (thinking to herself with hands on her head, her arms covering her eyes): No...No...No...this isn't true, this can't be true. Just the thought of losing them is too much for me. Call the number again and again and again...

Ian calls the number again,

THE NUMBER IS NOT VALID.

Lucy (yells): Call Mom and Dad. They called before right? Call on that number.

Leo (in shock): This is a lie, right? Lucy, Ian?

Lucy: This can't be happening. No, Not again. I have already lost my real parents before, I don't want to lose the parents who have helped me, raised me, and made me who I am right now. Hey, Ian, and Leo, I don't want to lose them...I..don't want to lose them. I will find and visit the place where they went on their 117th mission.

Leo (crying): I will come with you.

Ian (Head down): I will also come.

Lucy: It's a dangerous place since Mom and Dad were sent on the mission.

Leo: Earlier you said you were part of the group 'THE KILLER." Don't you have someone you can contact?

Lucy: I left the group when I went to college. They take everything when someone leaves the group. This is my new life and I don't want to waste a minute of it without my parents. Let's go and look for them.

Lucy was about to say something to her sentence, but Ian's phone rang.

RING...

RING...

Ian: Leo, Lucy - The phone call is from the mister.

Lucy: I don't want to talk to him right now.

Leo: Me too.

Ian: But...maybe he will know about our parents.

Ian picks up the phone.

The Mister: Hello, Kids. I am glad you completed your first mission. Now it's time for the second mission.

Leo (angry): Do you know where our parents are? If the answer is 'NO.' I don't think we are interested in doing missions for some unknown individual right now.

Ian and Lucy: Yes, We also think the same. We don't want to do any missions right now, and that too from an unknown individual.

The Mister: I know the location of your parents and I also know that I don't want to reveal myself so soon.

The Mister is about to say something but...

Ian stops him and says, "I don't want to know who you are...but...please...please tell me do you really know where our parents are and if anything has happened to them?

The Mister: If you finish the second mission by tomorrow night, then I will tell you about your parents.

Lucy (yells): BUT I WANT TO HEAR IT RIGHT NOW.

The Mister: Calm down, Lucy, if something has really happened to them, yelling will not bring them back. If yelling could bring someone back, I would have definitely considered it so many times in the past. So, now a question, Will you accept the mission? If yes, then one of you - RING THE DOOR BELL IN 1 HOUR.

BEEP...

BEEP...

THE PHONE CALL ENDS.

"SOMEWHERE"

Mr. and Mrs. Dellome are unconscious.

Around them, there are sixteen individuals and one of them is 'The Stranger' who was on the train with them.

Mr. Dellome wakes up and sees the stranger.

Mr. Dellome: You were with them this whole time, what do you want?

The Stranger: No, I wasn't and it's not what I want, it's what your leader wants.

Mr. Dellome: What do you mean by that?

The leader (in the dark): Now, Now, the mission is just starting, Mr. Dellome, let's wait, we still have 29 days to complete the real mission.

You know, Mr. Dellome, more than 18 hours have passed since you accepted this mission and you killed more than 100 individuals in less than 4 hours. Now I have only 14 individuals left. The individuals you killed were all trained assassins. I want to kill you two right now. But now it's time to tell you, what your mission really is.

Mr. Dellome: What do you mean by 'REAL MISSION?'

The Leader (in the dark): First, let's wait for Mrs. Dellome to wake up, then we can talk about the real mission, until then, have a good sleep.

SOMEONE HITS MR. DELLOME ON HIS HEAD.

.

.

MR. and MRS. DELLOME'S HOUSE

The time limit of 1 hour is about to end. Lucy, Ian, and Leo are discussing something.

Lucy: I don't trust him

Leo: Me too.

Ian: But we don't have a choice.

10 Minutes Left...

8...6..4...2 Minutes Left...

Leo goes outside and rings the doorbell.

Lucy: So, Ian, Leo, as discussed.

Leo and Ian: Yes, Yes.

RING...

RING...

Ian's phone rings.

Ian: Hello 'The Mister'

The Mister: So, after 58 minutes you decided to do the second mission.

Ian: Yes, we are, but before that, we want you to tell us about our parents. Where are they and what has happened to them?

The Mister: Let's start with ' Your parents are safe right now but I can't guarantee their safety for the next 29 days.

Lucy, Leo: OUR PARENTS ARE SAFE. Are you telling the truth? and What do you mean by the next 29 days?

The Mister: Yes, of course. I'm telling the truth. Their real mission will start in I don't know 'A FEW HOURS.'

Ian: Then why was the leader of the group ' THE KILLER' saying that?

The Mister: I don't know the answer to that question. So, now before you ask another question, I will give you the details of your second mission.

"GO TO THE DOOR. YOU WILL FIND A LETTER WITH THE DETAILS OF YOUR NEXT MISSION."

Leo runs to the door and finds the letter, picks up the letter, and rushes back with the letter in his hand.

The Mister: All the details of your next mission are written in that letter. Call me at the time mentioned in the letter.

Ian: Before that, I have one last question - WHO ARE YOU WORKING FOR?

The Mister: Maybe next time.

BEEP...

BEEP...

THE PHONE CALL ENDS.

.

.

Leo, Ian, and Lucy open the letter and in the letter, it was written:

> "*YOUR SECOND MISSION*
>
> *REACH THE A.F.T HOTEL AND WHEN YOU REACH THE HOTEL AFTER EXACTLY 1 HOUR, CALL 'THE MISTER.'*
>
> *EXAMPLE: SINCE YOU ARE KIDS - IF YOU REACH AT 7:00 A.M., CALL ME AT 8:00 A.M.*
>
> *YOU WILL GET FURTHER INSTRUCTIONS ON THE CALL. THE MONEY TO REACH THE HOTEL IS ALSO IN THE ENVELOPE. USE IT WISELY.*"

Lucy, Ian, and Leo are happy, their parents are alive.

Lucy: Pack your bags, let's finish this mission quickly. We have to wake up early tomorrow. The train will leave the station at 6:00 a.m. So we need to get ready by 5:30 a.m.

NEXT DAY

Leo: Hey, Lucy, Ian, Wake up, we have reached our destination.

CHAPTER SEVEN

TWO DIFFERENT MISSIONS, ONE FAMILY

NEXT DAY, 8:30 a.m.

Lucy, Leo, and Ian are waiting in the hotel. It took them fifteen minutes from the station to reach the market and then another half an hour to buy the things that were mentioned in the letter and another twenty to reach the hotel.

Leo: It's 8:30 a.m. now

Lucy: We can call the Mister now, right? Let's call him and finish this quickly.

Ian: No we can not. He mentioned in the letter that we have to wait for an hour before calling him.

SOMEWHERE

The Leader (in the dark): Hey you, are they awake? (pointing to someone from 14 individuals)

Someone from the 14 individuals: Yes Sir, they are awake, and Mr. Dellome is saying that he wants to talk to you alone first.

The Leader (in the dark): Alone...laughs...Bring both of them here. Let's start the real mission.

Someone from the 14 individuals: Sir, Do you really think they will accept the mission?

The Leader (in the dark): No, of course not, that's why I have something that will make them accept the mission.

After some time,

Mr. and Mrs. Dellome are in the room right now.

The Leader (in the dark): Since both of you are awake now, and are here, let's talk about the real mission.

The real mission is

THERE ARE 15 TRAIN STATIONS IN THIS CITY AND EACH STATION HAS A DIFFERENT LEADER.

Mr. Dellome: So, what do you want?

The Leader (in the dark): Listen to the full mission first.

THERE ARE 15 TRAIN STATIONS IN THIS CITY AND EACH STATION HAS A DIFFERENT LEADER. THEY NEED SOMEONE LIKE ME AS THEIR LEADER.

Mr. Dellome: What do you mean, someone like you?

The Leader (in the dark): You know, a leader like me who can use strategies and uses weapons only when the situation is fully out of control.

Mr. Dellome: Yes, of course, they need a leader like you, since you kept us alive. I believe that you have a calm nature. So, what do you need us for?

The Leader (in the dark): You know, just like us they also have people who work for them and they use weapons without thinking. Also, I have a question for you, do you know who this guy is (points laser light at the stranger)?

Mr. Dellome: Our leader said that he was an important person and told us to protect him at all costs.

The Leader (in the dark): First, let me tell you who this important person is, he is one of the weapon suppliers, and he supplies weapons to 7 of these 15 train stations, there is another weapon supplier but he left this city 1 year ago but still continues to supply the remaining train stations with weapons.

So, here is your mission - I want you to kill all the individuals in these 15 areas, don't worry there are no women and children in these 15 areas and if you still find one or two, just kill them, because if you don't, then they will kill you without thinking twice.

Mrs. Dellome - So, our mission is to kill these individuals with guns and ammunition. So, unlock these handcuffs now, and let's start this mission.

Mr. Dellome: Yes, open the handcuffs, we want to finish the mission soon and get back to our kids.

Mrs. Dellome: What about him? He is the one who supplies them with weapons.

The Leader (in the dark): Of course, I will open the handcuffs and don't worry about the kids, they are safe. But, first...

The leader was about to say something but...

Mr. Dellome (thinking to himself): How does he know about the kids? and stops him and asks, " How do you know about our kids and...

Mrs. Dellome: How do you know that they are safe?

The Leader: You know, Mr. and Mrs. Dellome, we needed something so I paid someone to follow and kill your kids if you declined the mission but since you accepted the mission easily, I will tell him to return.

HOTEL

Lucy: It's time. Let's call the mister right now.

Leo: Yes, let's call.

Ian dials the number

RING...

RING...

NO ONE IS PICKING UP THE PHONE.

A message pops up on Ian's phone, the message is from 'The Mister'

THERE WAS SOMEONE FOLLOWING YOU, HE IS IN THE ROOM NEXT TO YOU. TAKE HIM HOSTAGE, HE WILL BE THE KEY PLAYER IN HELPING YOU FIND YOUR PARENTS.

After reading the message, there is smile on the faces of Leo, Ian, and Lucy.

They are happy.

Lucy: Let's focus on catching this person as he can help us in finding our parents. Let's go to his room.

Leo: But what if he is strong, what if he has a weapon?

Lucy: Don't underestimate your sister, Leo, Ian. Why do you think boys stay away from me? Follow this plan.

Leo knocks on the door.

KNOCK...

KNOCK...

The person without opening the door says, "WHO?"

Leo: Cleaning Service, Sir.

The Person: But I ordered food, I need food, go and get me something to eat.

Leo: Yes Sir, the food you ordered is on its way too, but first we need to make sure that everything is clean.

The Person opens the door. Leo enters the room.

Leo: Starts cleaning the room and after some time starts whistling.

Lucy and Ian: Enter the room after hearing the whistle.

Lucy: Where is he?

Leo: In the washroom.

Lucy: Let's catch this guy.

The person returns from the washroom. Lucy and Ian who were waiting for him to come out, land a clean hit on his head with a wooden stick.

The person fell to the ground (unconscious).

Now Lucy was about to say something but the person's phone rang;

RING...

RING...

SOMEWHERE

Mr. Dellome (yells): If anything happens to my children, If you hurt them, I will kill every one of you. You better call the one who is following them and tell him to come back.

The Leader (in the dark): Yes, I am calling him and telling him to come back.

DIALS THE NUMBER AGAIN.

The Leader (in the dark): He is not picking up the phone. Here, I sent a message too.

HOTEL

RING...

RING...

What should we do

CHAPTER EIGHT

THIS OR THAT

RING...

RING...

The phone of the person is still ringing, Lucy and her brothers are discussing whether they should pick up the phone or not.

SOMEWHERE

The Leader (in the dark): The person who was following your kids is not picking up the phone. Maybe he is sleeping.

Mr. Dellome (yells): If anything happens to my kids, I will...

Mr. Dellome is about to say something but the Leader stops him and calls someone from the fourteen individuals.

The Leader (in the dark): Show him this message.

Someone from the fourteen individuals takes the phone to Mr. Dellome and shows him a message and then runs back to the leader.

The Leader (in the dark): Stop worrying, I have left the message that you just saw to that person, he will not harm your kids now.

Mrs. Dellome: Don't worry, Mr. Dellome, they have Lucy with them.

The Leader (in the dark): Lucy, is she your daughter, what will she do?

Mrs. Dellome: You will see it yourself one day.

HOTEL

The phone of the person stops ringing and a message pops up on the screen.

" THEY HAVE ACCEPTED THE MISSION. STOP FOLLOWING THE KIDS... AND COME BACK NOW."

Lucy sees the message and tells Ian and Leo about the message and says, "What should we do?"

Ian: Let's wait for this guy to wake up.

Leo: Let's send a message, 'COME BACK, WHERE?'

Lucy: No, I agree with Ian.

They take the person into their hotel room and tie him to a chair.

RING...

RING...

This time, it's Ian's Phone.

The call is from 'THE MISTER'

The Mister: Well Done. I never thought you will catch him. You three did a great job. But, now on to the mission. Did you buy the things that were mentioned in the letter?

Ian: Yes, we bought all the things. Now, tell us quickly what our mission is.

The Mister: Tell Lucy and Leo to bring these two items - 'A Book with a hardcover and many pages' and 'wires' with them to Room No. 12-B

Ian: I will come, too.

The Mister: No, only them. Wait for further instructions.

BEEP...

BEEP...

The call ends.

Leo: Why does he need these two things?

Lucy: Wires and A Book. Let's ask him directly.

Leo and Lucy tell Ian to take care of the person.

Ian: Don't worry about that. I will. He is unconscious.

ROOM NO. 12-B

There is no one in the room but there is a letter on the table. Lucy opens the letter and on it is written;

" LEAVE THE BOOK AND THE WIRE ON THE TABLE AND GO WAIT FOR 15 MINUTES OUTSIDE."

Lucy and Ian leave the book and the wire on the table and leave the room.

15...

10...

5...

1 Minute Left

10..9...8...7...6...5...4...3...2...1...Let's go inside.

Lucy and Leo enter the room again but to their surprise, there is neither the book nor the wires on the table.

Now, there is a knife and a gun with the note "CHOOSE ONE."

Lucy (yells): What were the wires and book for, then?

A message pops up on Leo's phone, it's from Ian, " CHOOSE ONE QUICKLY."

Leo (surprised to see the message): Why is he messaging me this?

Another message pops up on the screen, "10"

Another message "9"

Another message "8"

.

.

.

.

Another message "1"

.

.

RING...

RING...

Leo's phone rings and the call is from Ian.

Leo picks up the phone "We are about to cho..."

BOOM

A LOUD NOISE

Leo: What just happened?

Lucy: I heard a "BOOM" Was this from the mobile phone or...?

FOOTSTEPS...PEOPLE RUNNING...EMPLOYEES OF HOTEL RUNNING...OFFICIALS OF THE HOTEL RUNNING TO THE PLACE WHERE THE LOUD NOISE CAME FROM.

> "*A MESSAGE FROM THE OFFICIALS:*
>
> *PLEASE LEAVE YOUR ROOMS. THE FIRE IS SPREADING FAST. THREE ROOMS HAVE ALREADY CAUGHT FIRE. THEY ARE COMPLETELY DESTROYED. PLEASE GATHER IN THE WAITING AREA.*"

Leo and Lucy (shocked): They are still in Room No. 12-B. They don't know what to do. Should they visit their own room?

The employee comes and tells them to please gather in the waiting area.

He notices the tears in their eyes and asks them, "If someone close to you was residing in any of these rooms - Room No. 24-B, 25-B, and 26-B?

After hearing 25-B, they start thinking;

Maybe he ran before the blast.

Maybe he...

Maybe he...

Tears start rolling down from their eyes.

They don't know what they should do right now. What will they tell their parents? How will they face them now?

"*ANOTHER MESSAGE FROM THE OFFICIALS:*

PLEASE GATHER IN THE WAITING AREA QUICKLY. IT WILL TAKE TIME TO EXTINGUISH THE FIRE.""

IT TOOK THREE HOURS TO EXTINGUISH THE FIRE, THE AREA WAS SEALED. NO ONE WAS ALLOWED TO ENTER THE AREA.

.

.

SOMEWHERE

The Leader (in the dark): Points the laser light to someone from the 14 individuals

They want to finish the mission as soon as they can, open their handcuffs.

The Leader (in the dark): Don't try to do anything that will make me angry, Mr. and Mrs. Dellome. I still have the phone and I can still give new orders to the person following your children I just have to 'CALL' or press the 'SEND MESSAGE' button.

Mr. and Mrs. Dellome: Just open the handcuffs, let's finish the mission quickly.

Mr. Dellome: Do you have a map or something of...?

The Leader (in the dark): Yes, bring the map (to someone from the 14 individuals)

Mr. Dellome: We will need our weapons (guns and ammunition) back and a large wire.

The Leader (in the dark): Don't worry, we will provide you with everything. You just need to reach Station 1 first. When you are about 10 minutes away from Station 1, you will be provided with everything that you need for the mission there.

Mr. and Mrs. Dellome: Let's head to the station, then.

The Leader (in the dark): Yes, of course, but before starting the mission, we need to blindfold you guys, you know, precautionary measures..."

MR. AND MRS. DELLOME ARE BLINDFOLDED AND TAKEN TO THE PLACE FROM WHERE THE REAL MISSION STARTS.

WAITING AREA

Lucy and Leo are in the waiting area, the tears still rolling down their eyes.

Leo's Phone rings...

RING...

RING...

The call is from the Mister

Leo picks up the call.

The Mister: Sorry for that. Our boss wanted to have something so that you will not say 'NO' to the next mission.

Leo: What???

Lucy: Were you behind all this? I will kill you. Where is my brother?

Leo: We did everything you asked for. So, why...why...?

The Mister: Your mission was already over when you brought the books and the wire to that room but our boss wanted to extend the mission.

Lucy (yells): ALREADY OVER??? EXTEND THE MISSION? WHAT ARE YOU SAYING? IS THIS SOME

GAME FOR YOUR BOSS? MY BROTHER...? WHAT IS THE MEANING OF ALL THIS?

Leo: We will never accept the mission now. Don't call again. Your boss killed my brother.

The Mister: You know you have to, otherwise something bad will...

Leo: Something bad? What's left now? Will your boss kill us too?

The Mister: We did all this because we want you to accept the extended mission.

Leo and Lucy: But...But...You killed our brother, why...why would you do that?

The Mister: I want to tell you somet...

.

.

.

I felt emotional while writing the previous two chapters. Just the thought of losing someone close to me makes me emotional. I never want to lose someone close to me ever again.

CHAPTER NINE

WHO IS THE MISTER?

THE REAL MISSION STARTS NOW.

Mr. and Mrs. Dellome have reached their destination (10 minutes away from Station 1) where they will get everything they need for the mission. They are with 6 individuals and these individuals are taking them to an underground place.

Mr. Dellome: So, here is a list of things that we will need for the mission.

One of the Six Individuals: Out of these things, we will provide you with things that the leader approves of.

Calls the Leader.

RING...

RING...

The Leader picks up the phone.

The Individual: Mr. Dellome has given us a list of things that will help them in the mission, should we provide them with all the things they are asking for?

The Leader: Tell me the names of the things that they are asking for.

The Individual: These are the things they are asking for:

Wire
Guns
Ammunition
Knife
Map
Mobile Phone
Rope (with a hook at both ends)

The Leader: What do they need a mobile phone for? Calling their children? Leave the mobile phone and give them everything else.

The Individual: Okay, Leader.

BEEP...

BEEP...

The Phone Call ends.

The Individual (pointing his eyes to the other five individuals): Bring these things - Wire, Guns, Ammunition, Knife, Map, and Rope.

After some time, the five individuals return.

The Individual: Mr. and Mrs. Dellome, here are the things you asked for.

Mr. Dellome: I can't see a mobile phone in these things. Where is it?

The Individual: NO MOBILE PHONES ALLOWED, MR. DELLOME.

Mr. Dellome: If mobile phones aren't allowed, how will we contact the leader after completing the first mission?

The Individual: You don't need to worry about that, Mr. Dellome, three of our individuals will always remain in close contact with you two, of course, one of them will be hiding, since we know how strong you both are.

Mr. and Mrs. Dellome: Okay, then. Let's start the mission - Clearing Station 1.

The Individual: Stops Mr. and Mrs. Dellome and says "Do you have a plan? Infiltrating this place is hard. There will be individuals waiting or on the lookout.

Mr. and Mrs. Dellome: Yes, we have a plan. Just wait for three hours and if you are following us, maintain some distance or you will get caught in the crossfire. Let's meet again in 3 hours.

NEAR STATION 1

THE FIRST 10 MINUTES

So, Mrs. Dellome, are you ready?

Yes, Mr. Dellome, Let's finish this quickly.

Mr. Dellome is inside a small shed (looking out through the small gaps in the wooden boards)

Mr. Dellome: There are five individuals on the right and three on the left. You take the left, I will take the right.

Mrs. Dellome: No guns allowed, right, Mr. Dellome?

Mr. Dellome: Yes, Let's go.

Mr. and Mrs. Dellome take care of these eight individuals with ease.

Mr. Dellome: There is no one else here.

Mr. Dellome (continues): A PART OF MY HEART SAYS, " I DON'T WANT TO KILL THESE INDIVIDUALS BUT THE OTHER PART, IT IS SAYING, " SINCE ALL OF THEM HAVE WEAPONS AND HAVE KILLED HUNDREDS OF INNOCENT HUMANS AND CAN KILL US AT ANY GIVEN MOMENT, I WANT TO... I DON'T KNOW WHAT MY HEART WANTS TO DO TO THEM?"

Mrs. Dellome: If every weapon in this world was destroyed somehow, do you think the world...?

Mr. Dellome: One of the main reasons of why we started the group ' THE KILLERS'

Mrs. Dellome: Let's finish this mission. It's the same but I don't know how it will end. There is something I want to tell you. Let's move from here.

After covering some distance;

Mrs. Dellome: There are trackers in our shoes.

Mr. Dellome (shocked and yelling): TRACKERS, Why, When, How??

Mrs. Dellome: Don't yell. When we were asleep, I felt something and when I opened my eyes a little, I saw one of the individuals was putting the trackers in our shoes.

Mr. Dellome: That's the reason they were telling us not to worry about contacting them, they can find us at any time they want. I wonder who has?

Mrs. Dellome: I guess we will have to ask.

Mr. Dellome: Let's focus on the mission.

THE FIRST HOUR ENDS

33 INDIVIDUALS REMAINING

THE SECOND HOUR ENDS

16 INDIVIDUALS REMAINING

BEHIND A WALL

Mr. and Mrs. Dellome are behind two separate walls and

Mr. Dellome (yells): Hey, you remaining sixteen, do you really want to fight? If you saw what we did and what happened to the...

Someone from the sixteen individuals: Yeah, we saw what you did with the rope and the wire, but...

Mr. Dellome: I don't think you should fight anymore. Last Chance. I will count to three.

1...

WAITING AREA

Lucy and Leo (yelling): What...But...Why...KILLING OUR BROTHER?

The Mister: I really want to tell you something. Something...Something that happened three hours earlier. But, since both of you are yelling, those things can wait, and the next time I call make sure you both are in the right frame of mind.

Lucy (yell): What are you saying, Mister?

Leo(yell): The right frame...What do you mean by the right frame of mind?

Lucy: Do you really think we can be in our right frame of mind right now? Have you lost someone close to you, Mister?

The Mister (laughs): Lost someone close to me? I know it's a lot to take in, but here, I will tell you a story. Listen carefully.

Lucy and Leo: We're not interested in listening to your stories right now.

The Mister: Oh...it's the same. I know that feeling...I also had the same feeling when your parents (Mr. and Mrs. Dellome killed...) Let's not tell you about that part right now...You both are feeling the same as I was feeling on that day. Let's end this phone call here. I will tell you this story when we all are face to face and... about your brother...He is...

Lucy: Our brother is...

Leo: Our brother is...What about our brother?

BEEP...

BEEP...

The phone call ends.

.

.

Lucy: The Mister is behaving like a child, he is not telling us about our brother,...he is definitely hiding something from us...

Leo: I really don't know what to feel right now, what should we do..., what can we do?

Lucy: Let's go and see if we can find something in the rooms that were destroyed.

Leo: They were completely destroyed, and that area is sealed and so, how can we visit those rooms?

Lucy: I will talk with the person who told us to gather in the waiting area, if he says, "YES" then let's visit those rooms and hope that we find a clue..."

Leo: Yes...

....

UNKNOWN LOCATION

The Mister (yells): You punched me, how dare you?

The Boss: You don't know how to control your emotions and your mouth. You were about to tell them everything.

The Mister (yells): No, no...no, I wasn't. I am getting good at controlling my emotions. I just wanted to tell them about their brother.

A Slap.

The Mister (confused): Why...Why now?

The Boss: You know why. Tell them about their brother. Are you out of your mind? The brother is the key to the success of our plan and our plan will fail if you tell them about their brother.

The Boss: Let's put the next plan in motion and give Lucy and Leo their third mission.

The Mister: Okay, Boss.

.

.

HOTEL

After managing to get permission to visit the restricted area, Lucy and Leo are in an area that is restricted to everyone else.

Leo: Nice work, Sis.

Lucy: Thanks, brother.

Leo: There are three rooms. Let's see if we can find a clue...

Lucy: Yes, let's check these rooms one by one.

"***Room No. 24-B (The Stranger's Room)***

Leo and Lucy find nothing.

Room NO. 26-B (Someone's Room)

Find Nothing.

Room No. 25-B (Their Own Room)

Find A Burnt Mobile and A Burnt Finger With a Familiar Ring."

CHAPTER TEN

NO, NOT THIS AGAIN

THE RING, THE BURNT PHONE, and THE BURNT FINGER...

After seeing the ring, Lucy and Leo fall to their knees, tears rolling down their eyes.

> "*They don't know what to do and they are thinking of going to the police station.*"

The individual who gave Lucy permission enters the room and tells Leo and Lucy to leave the place quickly, the investigation team...

Leo and Lucy: But...

The Individual: You have to leave this area right now.

> "*They want to say something but they can't even move their lips. They don't know how to react or what to say.*
>
> *They are now in the waiting area.*
>
> *They are crying and suddenly Lucy stops crying...*"

Lucy: Hey Leo, Listen...(a gentle tap on the head)... Leo, do you...do you really think it's our brother's ring? As for me, I think that it's not our brother's ring. Hey, Leo, What...what do you think?

Leo who is in complete shock tries to say something but the words are not coming out of his mouth. It's like his lips are frozen.

FLASHBACK

Leo, Ian, and Lucy are on a trip with their parents.

They are walking in a forest-like area.

Ian asks his parents: Dad, I want to swim. Is there a lake or a pond nearby?

Dad: I am visiting this place for the first time, so I don't know if there is a pond or a lake nearby.

Mom: Let's search. If you find a pond or a lake, call us.

All of them go in different directions.

After some time, Ian hears HELP...HELP...SOMEONE HELP...MOM, DAD, LUCY, IAN.

Ian starts running towards the place where the sound is coming from.

Lucy and Ian arrive at the place.

Leo is yelling: Help, Help...Lucy, Ian, Thank God. Help me. I am dro...drown...drowning.

Ian is about to jump into the river but Lucy tells him to go and call mom and dad.

Ian: What if they arrive late, just wait, I know how to swim, I will save him.

Lucy: But...

Ian manages to save Leo.

Their parents arrive.

PRESENT DAY

Lucy: Let's call the mister again. I feel that he knows something about our brother.

Leo nods.

When Lucy tries to say something again, Leo (yells): I heard you, I'm not in the mood to talk right now. Please leave me alone for some time.

Lucy: Okay...Just don't do anything stupid.

Leo: starts walking in the waiting area.

.

.

UNKNOWN LOCATION

The Mister and The Boss are talking.

The Boss: Do you think those two can reach 'that' place by the time mentioned on 'that' thing?

The Mister: Don't you think 'that thing' burned in that huge fire and why...why aren't you telling me about your plan?

The Boss: Of course, not, "that thing" was not burnt.

The Mister: How do you know that?

The Boss: That thing was somewhere safe. It was not in the room and about the plan... I will tell you about the plan when those two reach 'that' place.

The Mister: What if they never find that thing? That's why I am telling you to tell me about the plan and also about the place where 'that thing' is and I will make sure that they find 'that thing' and reach 'that place.'

The Boss: Don't you have other things to worry about...Don't worry about that thing...focus on the thing I told you to do.

The Mister: Okay...Boss.

.

.

SOMEWHERE IN STATION 1

One of the three individuals who was following Mr. and Mrs. Dellome: You two must be exhausted after all that.

Mr. Dellome: Station 1 is clear, Now what?

The other individual: Our leader will be arriving at this place soon. He will tell you about the next mission himself.

Mr. Dellome: Oh, so he's coming here. I want to see who he really is.

Mrs. Dellome: Hey, you, (pointing to one of the three individuals), Do you think your leader really plans on expanding his territories or is he planning something else...?

No One responds.

Mr. Dellome: Forget that question. I have one question - Since all of these stations have one leader and above 100 individuals who know how to use weapons, there will come a time when we will meet someone stronger...

Mrs. Dellome (stops Mr. Dellome and): Someone stronger...? Someone stronger than us...?

Mr. Dellome: Yes, Someone stronger..., and what if we fail to win against him/her?

Mrs. Dellome: Also, since there will be so many of them, we will be exhausted, so we will need your help to clear all these stations.

One of the three individuals: That's why you two still have 26 days to complete the mission, and it depends on our leader, if he says 'Yes' then we will help you in this mission.

The Leader arrives but his face is covered with a mask.

The Leader: Thank you, Mr. and Mrs. Dellome for clearing Station 1, and as a token of appreciation, I have something I need to show you.

The Leader takes out his mobile phone and shows Mr. and Mrs. Dellome - A Photo.

The Leader: So, are you two happy now?

.

.

HOTEL

Lucy is sitting alone in the waiting area.

Leo comes and says, "Let's leave this place."

Lucy: Why, what happened?

Leo: That guy over there (pointing to a guy in a black hat) told me something, but first we need to leave.

Lucy and Leo are about to leave.

The individual at the counter stops them and tells them to take their things with them.

Lucy and Leo: All of our things are burnt.

The individual: Whose bag is this, then?

When Lucy and Leo see the bag, they are completely shocked.

Lucy: It's our bag...but...but how, this bag, it was in our room...the room that's completely burnt right now.

The Individual: You see that guy over there, the guy wearing a black coat, white shirt, and black jeans, he left this bag here with a message, "PAGE NO. 97" I don't know what that means, so you have to ask him.

Lucy and Leo take the bag and start advancing toward the guy but he starts running and disappears after entering a crowded street.

Lucy: What do you think, Page No. 97, means, Leo?

> "*Leo: I don't know the meaning of that, but the guy in the black hat told me,*
>
> *'You will receive a call from 'The Mister' when you reach the destination and there he will tell you about your brother."*"

SOMEWHERE IN STATION 1

Mr. and Mrs. Dellome: Why are you showing us this photograph, do we know this person, who is he?

The Leader (yells): Oh...So you don't know...Don't worry, I will tell you, he was the one who was following your children. They did this to him.

Mr. and Mrs. Dellome: Our children? Did this? Are you joking?

The Leader (yells): Joking... why do you think I am here? Do you know who he was?

Mr. and Mrs. Dellome: No, we don't.

The Leader: The message said that you will say this and then they also said that they are coming to kill me...you know...me...the leader.

Mr. and Mrs. Dellome: Can we see the message?

THE MESSAGE

HELLO, WHOEVER YOU ARE.

SEE THE ABOVE PHOTO. THE SAME THING WILL HAPPEN TO YOU.

TELL US WHERE OUR MOM AND DAD ARE AND WE WILL SHOW YOU KINDNESS BY NOT TREATING YOU THE WAY WE TREATED HIM.

REPLY SOON.

YOU HAVE 15 HOURS.

YOUR TIME STARTS NOW.

TICK...TOCK...TICK...TOCK...

Mr. and Mrs. Dellome: Start Laughing. I don't think that they wrote this message and if they did, someone is blackmailing our children.

The Leader: How can you be so sure?

Mrs. Dellome: Because we know them. They don't care about time. There is a proper time period mentioned in this message.

Mr. and Mrs. Dellome

ALSO, WE BELIEVE IN OUR CHILDREN. THEY WILL NEVER DO THIS. NOT TO THIS EXTENT.

Mr. Dellome: I have an idea. Send this message to the one who sent you this.

15 HOURS IS A LONG TIME. COME AND KILL ME RIGHT NOW.

BUT, SEND ME A PHOTOGRAPH, AS I NEED TO KNOW WHO IS COMING TO KILL ME.

The Leader: Mr. Dellome, don't you think that the ones who want to kill me will really come after reading this message.

Mr. Dellome: No, I don't think so. No one knows where you are, so, i don't think anyone will come.

Mrs. Dellome: But, if someone here is working for them, then...

Mr. Dellome: We can guarantee you one thing, they...

The Leader: Yes,...Yes, I know... Not your children...but...then...who sent this message?

Mr. Dellome: Since this message is from the mobile phone of the individual who was following our

children, I think someone else was following him. so this message is probably from that someone.

CHAPTER ELEVEN

THE REASON

The Leader: If someone else was following him, don't you think your children...

Mr. Dellome: I think the individual who was following him is protecting our children.

Mrs. Dellome: Someone from the...

Mr. Dellome (stops Mrs. Dellome): Yes, maybe...

OUTSIDE THE HOTEL

Leo: The place we need to go to is...

Lucy: Oh, this place... the map is showing it's 30 minutes away from here.

Leo: So, what are we waiting for? Let's go. The sooner we reach the place, the sooner we will know about our brother.

30 MINUTES LATER

Lucy and Leo: Let's wait for the call now.

Leo's phone rings.

Ring...

Ring...

Leo picks up the call.

The Mister: Well, well, you two. How are you, both?

Leo and Lucy: Tell us about our brother, right now.

The Mister: Before that, I have a question for you - who is the person behind you?

Leo and Lucy (look behind): There is no one. What are you trying to do?

Gunshot.

Lucy and Leo run towards the place where the noise came from.

Lucy and Leo: He is... He is the guy who gave us our bag and also, a clue - Page No. 97.

The Mister: I don't care about that. Check his pockets.

Lucy and Leo find a card - it's the identity card of the person.

Name - Mr. Kim

Works for - Y C NEGA

The Mister: oh, so he was the agency guy. Why was he following you, two?

Lucy and Leo: We don't know. But, you killed him, why?

The Mister: Look closely, there is a gun in his hand. He was about to shoot you guys and your safety is my concern right now.

Lucy and Leo: Shoot us, why?

The Mister: I don't know his reason. I have my own reasons to save you, two...

Beep...

Beep...

The phone call ends.

Footsteps...

Someone: Well, Well, they really reached this place. It's time for their third mission.

Lucy and Leo: Are you, Are you 'The Mister?' First, tell us about our brother. Where is he? What do you know?

Someone: Well, I'm not 'The Mister' so I don't know about your brother.

Lucy and Leo: Who are you, then?

Someone: Well, I'm "The Boss" I am the reason you did these missions.

Lucy: No, you are not the reason...

The Boss: Then, why are you doing these missions?

Lucy: Our Mom and Dad, and then our brother.

The Boss: But, it's not like your mom and dad are in any danger.

Leo: How do you know that?

The Boss: Well, I will tell you if you finish the third mission in less than 15 hours.

.

.

NEAR STATION 1

Mr. Dellome: Well, we cleared station 1 and we know that there are more than 10 stations still left, so...

The Leader: I know what you want, Mr. Dellome, he told me (pointing to one of the three individuals).

Mr. and Mrs. Dellome: So...?

The Leader: Well, there are 14 individuals, they know how to use weapons, and I will give you 10, they will follow you two.

Mr. and Mrs. Dellome: Okay, Great, Let's start our next mission "CLEAR STATION 2."

UNKNOWN LOCATION

The Boss: "Lucy and Leo, THIS IS YOUR THIRD MISSION."

GO TO STATION NO. 15

MEET THE LEADER

TELL HIM THAT SOMEONE IS COMING TO KILL HIM.

Lucy: What's with all this killing? What will you achieve by doing that?

The Boss: Well, it's not me who is going there to kill him, it's your mom and dad.

Lucy and Leo: They will never kill someone innocent, is this guy a bad person?

The Boss: Well, it's up to you two to decide if he's bad or not. To reach the place, you have to take two trains, one from here to Station Zero and then the other train from Station Zero.

.

.

.

.

.

.

.

SOMEWHERE

.

.

.

.

.

FAR

.

.

.

.

Someone is coming. Let's Go.

No, Wait.

I am going.

Okay, Done. Let's Go.

THE YEAR 2022.

Two players are playing chess.

Player 1 (using Black Pieces) - A 5-foot-7-inch old man (in his mid 40's) with curly hair and a mustache.

Player 2 (using White Pieces) - A 5-foot-5-inch old man (in his mid-50s) with some hair on his head and no mustache.

They are in the middle of their game when the arbiter (tournament director) suddenly stops the match and tells Player 1 to remain calm and come with him for a moment.

Chess Director: Sir. there is a message.

Player 1: A message??

Chess Director: Yes Sir, a message for you. The message is from an unknown number.

Player 1: Unknown Number.

Chess Director: Sir, someone has kidnapped your wife and daughter and...

Player 1: How do you know this message is for me? If it's how is this possible? (Points to his Manager - Give me my phone)

CALLS HIS WIFE

PICK UP...

PICK UP...

No one picks up the phone.

CALLS HIS DAUGHTER

PICK UP...

PICK UP

No one picks up the phone.

Player 1: Who did this, and why is this happening to me???

Chess Director: Sir, Please Stay Calm.

Player 1: What are you saying, how can I be calm? My Wife, My Daughter...

Chess Director: Sir, please read the message first.

Player 1: What do you mean, ‘ READ THE MESSAGE?’

Chess Director: You don’t have enough time, Sir.

Player 1: READS THE MESSAGE

IF YOU WANT YOUR WIFE AND DAUGHTER TO REACH THE HOUSE SAFE AND SOUND, JUST DO THIS.

AFTER LOSING THE MATCH AGAINST (NAME OF PLAYER 2), MAKE A VIDEO THAT YOU WILL NEVER PLAY CHESS AGAIN. IF YOU FAIL TO DO THE ABOVE-MENTIONED TASK, ONE OF THEM WILL DIE. YOU HAVE 30 MINUTES.

Chess Director: Sir, TIME LEFT - 25 MINUTES

Player 1 (in frustration) yells, " I AM IN A WINNING POSITION, HOW CAN I LOSE THIS MATCH?"

Chess Director: Sir, the police officers are on their way. Until then, just try to..."

Player 1: I know what you are trying to say but it’s not possible. I have a rook and a queen. Player 2 only has three pawns left. How can I?

Chess Director: If...Three Pawns - promote - Queen, Bishop, and Rook... Easily lose the match.

Player 1: I will try to... Just inform me as quickly as you can when the police officers arrive.

RETURNS TO PLAY THE GAME.

(On the way thinking)

Who will try to do this and why?

What will he/she achieve by doing this?

Reaches the table...

Player 2: Is everything okay, you seem...

Player 1: Yes, Yes... Everything is fine... Let’s focus on the game.

20 MINUTES LEFT...

Player 1 (thinking)

MY QUEEN IS ON f6

MY ROOK IS ON e1

MY KING IS ON c8

His King is on c2 and his pawns are on e3, g4, and h2.

I can easily win this game by moving my queen to c6. CHECK.

His king will move to b3, d2, or d3.

I can win in a few moves, but... I HAVE TO LOSE THIS GAME, so...

MOVES KING TO b7.

Player 2: Moves Pawn from h2 to h4.

Player 1: King to c6.

Player 2: Moves Pawn from g4 to g5.

Player 1: Moves Queen from f6 to f2.

Player 2: Is everything really okay?

Player 1: Yes, everything is okay, let's just finish this game.

Player 2: I just want to...

The Arbiter or The Chess Director interrupts again;

Sir, they are here.

Player 1: Oh...Let's go.

15 MINUTES LEFT...

Player 2 stands up and asks the arbiter or the chess director, " Is everything all right, Sir?"

Chess Director: Something has happened, you will know sooner or later, we can not say anything at the moment. (Walks away)

Player 1 reaches the office. The Police Officers are waiting for him.

Police Officer 1: Good Evening, Mr. Palm. The message that you received was from a nearby location. We sent two police officers there and we found nothing.

Mr. Palm: What do you mean by something?

Police Officer 1: We found a piece of paper on the table and there was another message for you.

Mr. Palm: WHAT, ANOTHER MESSAGE... WHAT WAS...

The police Officer interrupts Mr. Palm and replies

"I KNEW THE POLICE OFFICERS WILL COOPERATE WITH YOU. YOU ARE SPECIAL AND SINCE YOU ARE SPECIAL, YOU WILL RECEIVE A SPECIAL GIFT IN 10 MINUTES."

Mr. Palm: Since the moment you found this message, how much time has passed?"

Police Officer 1: Nine minutes, Thirty Seconds...31...32..."

Mr. Palm: In 20+ seconds, I will receive a gift.

40...

What...50...51..do...52...you...53...think...it...54...will...55....be?

Ring....56

Ring....57

Mr. Palm: Picks Up the Phone

58...59...60

Hel...Hello...Dad...Help...Dad

Mr Palm: Pam, Pam... Are you all right? Where are you?

Someone (on the other side of the phone): She is, right now. I don't know what will happen to her or your wife in the next 5 to 10 minutes.

Mr Palm: If anything happens to my wife and daugh...

Someone: Saving your wife and daughter is in your hands, Mr. Palm...if in the next 10 minutes, you fail to accomplish what I told you, something will happen to them and it will be on your hands. So, Mr. Detective... oh, I'm sorry Mr. Palm, it's up to you. THE TIME IS RUNNING OUT.

4 MINUTES LEFT.

TICK... TOCK...

TICK...TOCK...

The Phone Call ends.

Police Officer 1: Sir, try calling again.

Mr. Palm: I am trying. (puts the phone on speaker)

"THE NUMBER YOU ARE TRYING TO REACH IS CURRENTLY UNAVAILABLE."

Chess Director: Less than 4 minutes left, Sir.

Mr. Palm: Do you think I care about that right now, trace the last location.

Police Officer 2: Sir, we are already on that, the last location is RTS SCHOOL.

Police Officer 3: Distance.

Police Officer 2: 1 Kilometre.

Police Officer 1: Let's go.

Mr. Palm is also running towards the Police vehicle.

Police Officer 1: Mr. Palm, you have to stay here. We will call you as soon as we reach that place.

Mr. Palm: But...

Police Officer: We will contact you as soon as we find your wife and daughter. Please stay here.

Mr. Palm: ...

The Police Vehicles leave.

Mr. Palm (points to his manager): Tell the driver to bring my car.

Chess Director: Sir, 2 MINUTES LEFT.

Mr. Palm (about to say something)

THE PHONE RINGS.

RING...

RING...

Mr. Palm: Hello...

Police Officer 1: Sir, they are not her but there is another message, this time it is, " TICK... TOCK... TICK... TOCK...

and there are three dates."

> "*JUNE 21, 2007.*
> *SEPTEMBER 21, 2007.*
> *DECEMBER 21, 2007.*"

Mr. Palm (yells in frustration): WHAT DO THESE DATES HAVE TO DO WITH ANYTHING? WHAT IS HE/SHE TRYING TO DO?

Police Officer 1: Sir, do you remember anything?

Mr. Palm: Just one date seems familiar - JUNE 13, 2007. My final tournament match was on this date.

Police Officer 1: Sir, we found nothing on the web, do you recall which match?

Mr. Palm: A 20-Million Dollar Prize Money Match.

Police Officer 2: Sir, we found a news article dated June 14, 2007, and the title is...

Mr. Palm: PALM QUESTIONED. IS HE ONE OF THEM?

Police Officer 2: Huh... What's this article about?

Mr. Palm: There was a tournament. We were forty players (including me) and we received letters. The time and the place where the tournament would take place were mentioned in the letter.

It was not an ordinary chess tournament. It was held in a three-story mansion with an underground basement. All the matches took place in that underground basement and when someone lost, he was sent through the door of that underground basement and that player was never seen again. After the first five matches...

Police Officer 1 (stops Mr. Palm): Sir, I understand that. But the article is about how some police officers questioned you and everyone in your family about the theft of 100 million dollars.

Mr. Palm: At that time, some police officers believed that the money transferred to my bank account was 'THE STOLEN MONEY' and...

Chess Director (stops Mr. Palm): Sir, only 2 minutes left.

Police Officer 1: Sir, you should focus on the match.

Mr. Palm (in frustration) yells: HOW CAN I?

> "*MY WIFE AND DAUGHTER. THEY ARE... I DON'T KNOW WHERE... I ONLY HAVE ONE CHOICE - I HAVE TO LOSE THIS GAME.*"

Police Officer 1: We will try our best to find your wife and daughter.

BEEP...

BEEP...

The Phone Call Ends.

Chess Director: Sir, 2 minutes left.

Mr. Palm (thinking to himself): I need to find my wife and daughter myself.

(STARTS RUNNING)

Chess Director: Sir, this would mean...

Mr. Palm: I know what this means and I don't think I have a choice here.

After 2 minutes

THE CHESS DIRECTOR ANNOUNCES: The winner of this tournament is Player 2 - Mr. Jab.

.

.

.

AFTER 10 MINUTES;

Mr. Palm reaches his house.

Opens the door. Enters his house. Someone is sitting on the couch. Mr. Palm can not see him/her.

"WE TOLD YOU NOT TO MENTION ANYTHING ABOUT THAT TOURNAMENT."

Mr. Palm: I just told them...

"WE KNOW WHAT YOU SAID TO THE POLICE OFFICERS ON THE PHONE CALL."

Mr. Palm: Please don't hurt my wife and daughter. I will never say anything again regarding...

"WE NEVER KIDNAP. YOU KNOW THAT - MR PALM, DON'T YOU?"

Mr. Palm: So, who kidnapped them?

"WE DON'T KNOW THAT. WE CAME HERE TO ASK YOU THIS QUESTION - (THROWS A PHOTOGRAPH) - DO YOU KNOW WHERE THIS PERSON IS?"

Mr. Palm: No, I...

SOMEONE HITS HIM ON THE HEAD.

After 3 Hours;

THE MEDIA IS OUTSIDE Mr. Palm's house and the police officers are now searching for Mr. Palm, his wife, and his daughter.

BREAKING NEWS

MR PALM, HIS WIFE, AND HIS DAUGHTER HAVE DISAPPEARED.

THANK YOU FOR READING.

.

.

.

PART 2 OF "THE IDENTITY"

AND

THE MANSION (UNSOLVED MYSTERY)

.

.

SOON

9 798889 599951

Printed by Libri Plureos GmbH in Hamburg, Germany